Fantasy Short Stories

By

Suzanne Rogerson

DEDICATION

I would like to dedicate these stories to my readers.
Thanks for all your support.

TABLE OF CONTENTS

THE GUARDIAN

'It's good to see you Cassima, but this isn't just a friendly visit,' Kalesh said as he nursed the cup of herbal tea and faced his former student across her kitchen table. It was a homely space with bundles of herbs hanging from the rafters and the smell of freshly cooked bread scenting the air. The cottage was adequate to raise a family, but poor protection against the evil he feared would track her down.

'The assassin is targeting our people. Out here you're at his mercy. You need to move closer to civilisation.'

'My magic guards us.' Cassima answered him quickly, as though she'd been rehearsing the speech.

He held back a retort as he pulled Cassima's daughter onto his lap and took the small posy of flowers the child offered him. 'Thank you, Varnia.' He stroked a purple petal, recalling the healing qualities of the bloom.

'They grow by the lake. Mummy lets me pick them, but not too many so they keep coming back,' Varnia told him wisely.

He smiled at the youngster and looked at the pregnant woman opposite. Despite Cassima's bravado, a trace of fear showed in her eyes; she never could disguise her true feelings from him.

'Why don't you go and play, Varnia,' her mother said.

He felt a flair of magic in the child as she slipped from his lap and ran outside.

'Don't go far,' Cassima called after her.

'Yes, Mummy.'

Kalesh glimpsed the clearing through the open door and watched the child running through the meadow of colourful wildflowers and swaying grasses. He threaded his fingers together, noting the ink-stains on his skin, before meeting Cassima's defiant gaze. 'You can't hide Varnia forever; the Royal Wizards will find out about her power and want to train her.'

'They're not taking my daughter away.' She rubbed her belly. 'I won't let them take either of my children.'

'It's the assassin you should be worrying about. You'll be safer at the castle.'

'No!'

'He's systematically killing us off. Out here I can't protect you.'

She shook her head. 'I can protect myself.'

'Cassima why do you have to be so stubborn?'

'I had a good teacher.' For an instant she was the teenager under his tutelage again; she never listened to his advice then either.

Cassima's expression softened as she reached across the table and squeezed his hand. 'You can find him, master. I know you can stop him.'

'We're trying, but he's like a ghost.' He fell silent, picturing the friends he'd already lost. So much ancient knowledge gone forever, and for what? They didn't understand the murderer's motives and that's what made it difficult to judge his next move or predict the next target. When Kalesh realised Cassima could be on the assassin's list, he knew he had to persuade her to abandon her solitary life.

Cassima rose and stood in the doorway smiling as she watched her daughter chasing butterflies.

'I can see she's happy here,' he said reluctantly as he joined Cassima.

'I don't want Varnia to suffer the same regime I did. I want her to be free, to have friends, to love. If the Royal Wizards got hold of her, she'd be trained as their tool.'

Kalesh paced the length of the room, floorboards creaking beneath his feet. 'You're asking me to leave you here, to risk the assassin finding you.'

'Yes.' Her protection ward around the cottage rippled and tightened in response.

'There's no denying you're skilled but think about the wizards he's already killed; they were just as powerful as you are.'

'But I've been hidden for a long time, you saw to that.'

Kalesh shook his head. 'It might not be enough. At least bring your family to Hawthorn Cottage. United we have a chance.'

'And how would you explain our presence to the wizards, to the baron, to your new charge?'

'The wizards don't care what happens on the outskirts of Paltria and Baron Harkai is an understanding man. Paddren is a quiet lad, but he'd love the company. Given the chance, he and Varnia could be friends.'

'No, Kalesh I'm sorry. This is how it must be. You should go, my husband will be back soon.'

He hugged her. 'You've always been my favourite student, even if you were the most stubborn.'

Laughter lines creased her face and gave light relief to the worried expression ageing her prematurely. 'And you were always my favourite tutor. But you need to let your students go. Paddren, needs your guidance now.'

He thought of the boy in his care and couldn't shake the notion that somehow it was all connected. The boy and his visions, the assassin…

Outside the cottage, Varnia ran over when she saw him head towards his tethered horse. Little sparks of magic flashed in her bright blue eyes as she hugged him.

'Goodbye Uncle.' She waved and was off again, a whirlwind with blonde hair and a cheeky grin.

Kalesh looked back at the small, secluded cottage and prayed it would remain her sanctuary for a long time to come.

He passed Cassima a gold hawthorn brooch. 'Contact me with this talisman if you need me.'

She nodded and slipped the brooch into her pocket.

He mounted his horse and stared down at Cassima. Magic pulsated from her, stronger and more focused with the pregnancy. 'Take care of your family.'

'I will.' A ghost of a smile tugged at her lips. 'Look after your new charge, I sense he'll be important.'

Kalesh pictured the youngster he'd rescued from the Royal Wizards. 'Yes, I believe he is.'

'Where is he now?'

'With the hunt master. Reaun planned to teach him to ride a pony and fight with a sword.'

'Reaun's a good teacher. Between the two of you, Paddren will thrive as I did.'

'We'll do our best. Goodbye, Cassima. I'll visit again soon.' Kalesh led the gelding onto the path through the trees and headed for Herristone. He muttered the words of the spell to mask his tracks, feeling it settle on the earth in his wake.

They trotted through the forest, taking a more leisurely pace than usual while he pondered Cassima's decision to stay away from the Royal Wizards. Their stifling control had tarnished her view of the magical community in Paltria, but to risk herself and her children…

As he held the posy of flowers Varnia had given him, he saw a glimpse of the future – a warrior woman with a hardness in her intense blue eyes. One day Varnia would lose her childhood innocence, he just hoped the life lessons were not too harsh.

Birdsong eased into his troubled thoughts, forming a soothing backdrop to the journey. He patted his horse and picked up the pace as they left the forest behind.

Cassima was right about one thing, Paddren needed a guiding hand. Suffering and hurt lay heavily on his young shoulders. There had been no love in his life since the day he thought his family abandoned him at Kranor Castle. It could not be further from the truth, but the Royal Order insisted on detachment to ensure a wizard's devotion to the magic and their king. Allowing the lie to stand meant Kalesh was no better than his comrades. He sighed, cursing the difficult choices he must make to keep Paddren safe.

The subtle touch of telepathic contact disrupted his trail of thought. *Fenook.* He greeted his old friend.

How did you fair with Cassima?

Not good, she's refusing our help. We must find the assassin, it's the only way to keep them safe. Kalesh felt distress leaking through the link with his friend. *What's wrong Fenook?*

There was another murder. An apprentice guardian this time.

Were there any witnesses?

None we could find.

I hate this farce of a role I play. Barony wizards have no power or influence. I hate being blind and helpless in this battle, Fenook.

There was a pause. He imagined his friend worrying at his beard. *We're all doing our best to trace the killer, but he's adept at covering his tracks. I believe it's a fellow wizard turned against us.*

I suspect the same. But who, and why?

Kalesh, leave the assassin to us. You have more important work to contend with.

What about Cassima and her daughter?

We'll do all we can to keep them safe. You must look after the boy, find out the meaning behind his visions. You must protect him at all costs.

I'll do whatever it takes. Kalesh ended the conversation and kicked his heels into the gelding's sides eager to get back to Hawthorn Cottage and his charge. He'd already been gone too long.

***

'I've had a new vision.' Paddren rushed out to greet Kalesh as he rode into the garden surrounding Hawthorn Cottage.

The lad had a red lump and graze on his forehead. A jolt of concern rushed through Kalesh as he slipped from the saddle to examine Paddren.

Reaun followed the youngster outside, looking apologetic. 'We were riding in the woods when he fell off of the pony. Lucky you have a thick skull.' Reaun ruffled Paddren's hair affectionately and the boy responded with a shy smile. 'The pony must've been spooked by something, but he was a brave lad and got straight back on.'

Kalesh eyed Paddren, satisfied he was otherwise unhurt though the boy had a haunted look. How bad could this new vision be?

'I'll deal with the horse for you.' Reaun took the reins of Kalesh's gelding and led it to the small stables at the back of the cottage, trailed as always by his faithful hound. It wasn't Reaun's job, but his friend loved horses and dogs as much as he loved being hunt master at Redstone Manor.

'The vision made me fall off. It wasn't Master Reaun's fault.' Paddren's quiet words drew him back to the present. The boy stared at the ground, playing with the signet ring on his finger.

Kalesh's own fingers twitched with the urge to record the vision in his journal, but he forced himself to be patient. From experience he knew

Paddren needed to be in a relaxed state if he was to recall all the details and allow Kalesh to draw out every nuance of the vision.

'Why don't we have some supper and then you can tell me about your vision when the hunt master has gone home?'

His charge nodded, still eager to please his new master and avoid going back to Kranor Castle. Kalesh didn't know what the young boy had suffered there, but he sensed it was more than the callous disregard of the Royal Order. They saw the boy's lack of magical bloodline and inept skills as a liability, Kalesh saw them as his strength. Especially with an assassin in their midst.

They ate roast hare, courtesy of Reaun's traps, and vegetable stew while they talked about Paddren's day of sword practice and riding. Afterwards they waved Reaun off before settling in Kalesh's study with a roaring fire to chase away the gloom of dusk.

The youngster sat in the chair opposite and rubbed his fingers across the emblem on his signet ring. Paddren still drew strength from the family crest even though he believed they'd disowned him.

Kalesh opened his journal, picked up his quill and inked the nib. 'When you're ready,' he said gently.

The incense in the room created a smoky haze and Paddren sank back in the seat, resting his head against the wood as he closed his eyes. His breathing slowed and his tensed features relaxed reminding Kalesh how young Paddren was to be laden with such a burden.

'I'm in the same broken city I always see. This time wizards are gathering around a pyre made of books and scrolls. There must have been a battle because the buildings are rubble and there are bodies…' He paused to take a breath his eyes still screwed shut.

The hairs on the back of Kalesh's neck stood on end as he scribbled it down. 'It's alright, Paddren. Tell me what else you remember.'

'They put a body on the pyre, a man. Wizards perform rituals over him, but I can't understand their words. I think the dead man is their enemy, though they don't look happy about his death. The wizards join hands forming a circle. One wizard speaks and the books catch fire. It rages hot, licking over the body.

'When the dead man is burnt to ash everyone leaves. Only one wizard stays behind, the one in the red cloak who started the fire. He sweeps up the remains in a fancy urn. Then he stands and looks at me. He whispers my name. I still hear his voice in my head…' Paddren shuddered and sat upright, the connection to his vision lost.

Kalesh set down the quill and rubbed his temples. He took a toke on his pipe and leant back in the chair. Releasing the smoke on a long, slow breath his tension dissipated. His body was achy and stiff from the ride but in his mind, clarity began to form.

'You did well, lad.' He regarded the youngster as Paddren shifted in the chair opposite. 'I know these visions are hard for you to relive but the more I understand them, the better I will be able to help you control them. You see that, don't you?'

'Yes, Master Wizard.'

'Good. Now get to bed and we'll talk more in the morning.'

Kalesh watched Paddren go before re-reading the words he'd transcribed. The answers were there somewhere, waiting for discovery. He read back through the dozen journal entries he'd made since he rescued Paddren from Kranor Castle. Each vision seemed to link to the past, he just had to decipher how and why.

A piece of paper wedged in the book caught his attention and he pulled it free. He traced the ink outline of the creature. Paddren's crude drawing of a Nagra was all claws and fangs but he'd captured the evil essence in its blood-red eyes.

People believed the terrifying creatures were myths; Kalesh knew better. Nagras were conjured by blood magic, but only the most powerful sorcerers could perform the spell and the information was a closely guarded secret.

It was the drawing that had given Kalesh the first inkling of how special Paddren was. A higher force had seen the latent talent in the child and now it was Kalesh's task to discover what it all meant.

Securing the picture back within the pages of his journal, he stored it in his desk and sealed the drawer with a spell.

He stood at the window, viewing the cottage garden as it shone in the twilight.

Kalesh felt the shifting of fate around the lad. Something important was happening in Paltria and Paddren was at the heart of it.

He couldn't let the assassin discover him. He would hide and protect the youngster until Paddren was strong enough to face whatever destiny had planned for him.

The path ahead would be difficult for them both, but he suspected Paddren had the heavier burden waiting in his future.

***

You can find out what happens to Paddren and Varnia in the standalone epic fantasy, Visions of Zarua.

Read on for the first chapter of Visions of Zarua…

VISIONS OF ZARUA

CHAPTER ONE

*He stood outside the broken entrance of the citadel
and watched the small pyre burn. Bright flames
licked high into the night sky and smoke drifted on
the breeze, carrying the stench of burning flesh.
Twigs crackled and a log split, sending sparks
spiralling upwards. The contents of the inferno
shifted, giving a glimpse of the blackened limbs
within...*

Paddren shook himself from the grip of the
vision, though the smell of smoke clung to his
nostrils and his skin felt clammy from the heat. He
massaged his temples as he strode through the
market square and made his way to the stall selling
herbs.

The leathery-faced stall owner caught his gaze
and gave a discreet nod. While the trader continued
to gossip with another customer, Paddren sorted
through the herbs and spices, picking his usual
assortment of foreign plants that wouldn't grow in
the colder climates of Paltria. Among them were
dried luca leaves from the distant shores of Seya
and a tiny jar of dried starspike flowers from
Paltria's neighbours in the western borderland of
Cazonia. He added a small sack of tobacco to his
collection before searching through the myriad of

fresh cut leaves for purple lentah, the potent herb that grew on the harsh northern shores of Paltria. He picked up a bunch of wilting stems and sniffed them. The herbs had curled at the edges and only a faint hint of peppery scent remained.

'You're getting careless,' Paddren said as he handed his selection to the stallholder.

'It'll be fresher next time, I promise.' He offered Paddren an earnest smile, all gums and crooked teeth. 'Take an extra ounce of tobacco and tell Master Kalesh it comes with my warmest regards.'

Paddren rolled his eyes and pocketed the tobacco. He watched the hawker's hands wrap the purchases in a large square of linen and nodded when the trader slipped a pouch into his palm beneath the package of herbs.

'I take care of everything.' The man grinned.

Paddren tucked the linen parcel amongst the other supplies in his pack, while the pouch disappeared into a hidden pocket of his cloak. He counted out payment, adding an extra coin to ensure the herb-seller's continued silence.

'See you next month, Master Kalesh's apprentice,' the stall owner said with a wink.

Paddren nodded and headed back into the bustling crowd. He patted the small pouch of herbs concealed in his cloak as he threaded his way through the market. The pungent smell of plants gave way to the appetising aromas of hog roast and meat pies, reminding him that he'd missed breakfast.

'Try a bunton cake, freshly made today…'

'Sample the finest honey cakes in all Paltria…'

Rival stallholders filled the air with shouts as they competed for passing trade. Paddren allowed their friendly jousting to wash over him and headed for the stables. As he stepped through the unmanned gates of the Redstone Manor estate, a presence shrouded by darkness brushed against his mind. Sharp pain ripped through his skull and white light flashed across his vision. He staggered to a halt and dropped his pack of supplies on the cobbles as a thunderclap exploded in his head. He gripped his skull between his hands, the pain so excruciating he had to clench his teeth to stop from screaming. His mental shield began to buckle, but then the unfamiliar presence retreated as suddenly as it had arrived.

He sucked in a shaky breath and tasted the tang of blood in his mouth. A tremor quaked through his body and his hand shook as he stooped to snatch up his discarded bag.

'Are you all right, Paddren?' one of the baron's stewards asked, detaching himself from the small crowd that had gathered to watch.

'I'm fine,' Paddren said, forcing a smile.

The onlookers began to shuffle away. Ignoring them, Paddren tried to envisage the dark presence - certain it had been searching for someone or something. Whatever its purpose, he knew he had to tell his master.

He hurried to the stables and caught the stable boy dozing in the straw. He tapped the lad's foot.

'Sorry, Master Wizard, sir,' the boy stuttered.

Paddren paced the aisle between the stalls while he waited for the lad to remove the empty feedbag and fumble with the girth straps.

'That'll do.' Paddren tugged at the saddle horn and climbed onto his horse. He flipped the lad a coin and then turned the mare's head and bolted out the stable door. They tore across the courtyard and out the manor gates, scattering several people from their path. 'Sorry,' he called over his shoulder.

Switching the reins into his right hand, Paddren searched inside his shirt pocket and gripped the gold talisman brooch.

Kalesh. He reached out telepathically, but something was blocking their link.

On the outskirts of Herristone, Paddren kicked his heels into the mare's flanks and galloped across the open ground. He continued to press the horse in a brutal dash through the forest that separated the town from Hawthorn Cottage. The miles of beech trees seemed to stretch for an eternity, but finally he broke through the shade of the woods and crossed the clearing towards the oak-framed cottage he called home. Its thatched roof stuck out above the fence of hawthorn bushes, which were just shedding the last of their creamy-white blossom. He charged his horse through the open gate and frowned as he noticed the closed cottage shutters and smokeless chimney. Vaulting from the saddle, he dumped his supplies by the door and gave the garden a cursory glance.

'Master Kalesh!'

Seeing no sign of his master, or their servant Leyoch, he rushed inside the cottage. The hearth in the main room was swept clean and the breakfast things all tidied from the table. The three bedrooms were empty, and Kalesh's study door was locked - something he only did when he was going out.

Paddren was certain there had been no suggestion of Kalesh going anywhere when he'd left the two men relaxing over their morning brews.

He slumped into a chair by the unlit fire and took a deep, calming breath. Pulling the brooch from his pocket, he traced the hawthorn design that was worked into the precious metal. Closing his eyes, he stroked the golden brooch with his thumb.

Master, where are you?

Be gone, lad, this is not your concern, the wizard answered after a long pause.

Paddren grappled after their faint connection and immediately sensed the dark presence shadowing his master. *Master Kalesh, there's a malevolent spirit...*

I know. I'm trying to protect you from it you fool. Now go.

I won't leave until you tell me what's going on.

I command you to leave now!

A barrier slammed between them.

Paddren's eyelids fluttered open and he found himself sprawled on the floor. Forcing down the sour taste of nausea, he stashed the talisman back in his pocket and climbed to his feet, then stumbled to the door of the cottage and leant against the oak frame, waiting for his throbbing head to clear. Instead, the garden blurred as another vision slipped past his resistance.

...the chair toppled and clattered to the floor. A man dangled from the exposed beam, his legs kicking wildly as he clawed at the rope tightening around his neck. In the shadows, a hooded figure watched until the death throes stopped and the man's body hung limp...

Paddren squeezed his eyes shut and tried to push the vision from his thoughts. He ducked back inside the cottage and grabbed the sword from under his bed, then dashed outside and whistled to his horse. She came at his call and snorted as he tied the sword to his saddle-roll and remounted. From the new vantage point, he reached out with his magic to trace Kalesh's route, but a blocking spell masked his master's presence beyond the gates of Hawthorn Cottage.

'You're a stubborn old fool, Kalesh,' Paddren muttered as he nudged the mare onto the path that led back to Herristone.

***

A chill ran through Varnia. She glanced at her hounds, dozing in the sunlight that broke through the canopy of luminous beech leaves. The forest trilled with birdsong and a warm breeze ruffled the air.

'Are you cold?' Leyoch traced his fingers across her belly. 'Because I know a way to warm your blood.'

She pushed his hand away and sighed.

'Stay a bit longer, it's not often we're both given the morning off.'

'I should get back before someone notices.'

'You just can't take the pace.' Leyoch smirked at her, and then sat up and reached for his clothes.

Varnia propped herself up onto her elbow and watched him pulling on his breeches, enjoying the view of his muscled back still glistening with sweat.

'If I didn't have to masquerade as Reaun's niece, we wouldn't have to sneak around like this,' she said.

He twisted to face her and his brown eyes sparkled with passion. 'Are we not happy in these stolen moments?'

'Of course, but it still feels tainted by what I can't have.'

Her restless fingers tugged through the thick, wiry coat of the hound lying next to her. Flint rolled onto his side allowing her to rub his belly and she smiled at the deerhound's laziness.

Compelled by thoughts of their inevitable parting, Varnia slipped on her leggings and boots, and buttoned up her long-sleeved tunic. Then she pulled on her leather waistcoat, but lingered over the fastenings. She flopped back on Leyoch's cloak and stared into a patch of clear sky between the towering silver-grey trunks. The sun's position warned her she was already late returning to the manor.

'When can you get away next?' he asked as he laced his boots.

'I'm not sure.' She trailed her fingers through the dried leaf litter, feeling the dusty red soil beneath. It hadn't rained for weeks. Reaun had said it was the driest spring he could remember.

Both hounds stood, their ears pricked forward as they stared into the forest. Varnia registered the vibrations through the earth. 'Someone's coming!'

They leapt to their feet. Varnia's heart pounded as she trapped her long hair in a clumsy braid and smoothed down her clothes. As she strapped on her knife belt, she watched Leyoch shake his cloak free of dust before stuffing it into his pack. He met her gaze and, on impulse, she blew him a kiss, glad for the brief smile he gave in return.

The horseman rode into sight. Varnia recognised Paddren and grinned with relief as her friend reined in his horse. But her smile faded as she noticed his dishevelled hair and clothes. His dark eyes scanned the forest before he glowered down at her. Varnia braced herself for Paddren's reproach.

Instead, Paddren turned to Leyoch. 'Where's Kalesh?'

He shrugged. 'How should I know? It's my morning off.'

'Then I need your help now, Varnia.' Paddren directed the full intensity of his stare on her. 'Follow me.'

She opened her mouth to protest, but Paddren had already turned his horse and galloped down the path. She stared in disbelief at his retreating back. 'What was that about?'

'We'd better follow him and find out.' Leyoch slung his pack over his shoulder and sprinted after the disappearing wizard.

Varnia signalled to her hounds and set off in pursuit. The burn of exertion coursed through her sluggish limbs and she cursed. If she hadn't had to sneak away, she would've had her horse.

**

Paddren pumped the reins, furious at the time he'd wasted searching for Varnia. All the while, she'd been enjoying another secret assignation in the woods. He tried to push the thought from his mind and eased up the pace.

'Paddren, wait.'

He pulled his mare to a halt.

'What's wrong?' Varnia asked when she eventually caught up with him.

Paddren saw the concern crease her brow and his temper softened. 'Kalesh is in trouble, but he's blocking me. I need you to track his route from the cottage.'

'You could've said that in the beginning.'

'I know. Sorry.' He held out his hand and pulled her up onto the horse behind him. Flicking the reins, he trotted along, leaving Leyoch to jog beside them.

At Hawthorn Cottage, Paddren waited outside the gate for Leyoch to retrieve his horse from the stable.

Varnia slipped down from the saddle and studied him with her tracker-sharp eyes. 'Your agitation is upsetting her,' she said, reaching out to stroke the mare's neck.

Paddren relaxed his shoulders and sighed. 'I can't break Kalesh's blocking spell.'

'Then stop trying. You know you can trust me to find him.'

He managed a half-hearted smile. 'Varnia, whatever's going on, this involves wizards and it could be dangerous. You and Leyoch must promise to turn back when I say.'

Before she could reply, Leyoch emerged from the stables and led the saddled stallion towards them.

'Hello Shadow.' Varnia rubbed the horse's black nose and he nuzzled her hand in greeting.

Leyoch offered her the reins, but she waved them away and raised her eyebrows at the sword now strapped at his side.

'I'll go and find Kalesh's trail,' Varnia said and ran to join her hounds who were already sniffing around outside the cottage.

'You don't need a weapon,' Paddren said.

'He's my master, too. I want to help.'

Paddren sighed, intending to give Leyoch the same warning he'd given Varnia, but something in the way Leyoch mounted his horse and stared off into the distance drew his suspicion. 'Are you sure you don't know where Kalesh has gone?'

Leyoch shrugged.

Paddren narrowed his eyes, but before he could continue his questioning, the hounds began to bark.

'I've found his tracks.' Varnia ran back to join them. 'It was difficult to trace, as though Kalesh wanted to disguise them. I only spotted them because he was accompanied by another rider and a hound.'

They both turned to Leyoch, who was picking at the pommel of his saddle. 'Hunt Master Reaun visited this morning just as I was leaving.'

'But he told me he was setting traps in the Western Woods,' Varnia said. 'What's going on, Leyoch?'

'I assumed Reaun stopped by to wish Kalesh a safe journey.'

'He made no mention of a journey to me,' Paddren interrupted.

Leyoch gazed at the ground. 'I don't know any details. I wasn't supposed to mention it until this evening.'

'I can't believe he would keep this from me. What other secrets have you and Kalesh been hiding?'

Varnia barged between their horses and glared up at them both. 'This isn't the time to argue. If my master is with Kalesh, he could be in danger too.'

Paddren watched her signal to the hounds and jog after them. He followed, trotting his horse alongside Leyoch.

Once the trail was established, Varnia joined Leyoch on Shadow's back and allowed the hounds to lead the hunt. Several miles into the forest, she called for a halt and examined the tracks.

'They stopped here. The horses seem agitated, as if their riders were arguing.'

'I've never seen those two share a cross word,' Paddren said.

'Well, that's what it seems like.' Varnia kicked her heels into Shadow's sides and resumed the chase.

Less than a mile later, she forced them to stop again and jumped down from the saddle. 'They were definitely arguing.'

'We don't have time for this, Varnia.' Paddren clenched his teeth and twisted the reins in his fists.

Without warning, the presence reached out to him. He recoiled from its malevolent touch and strengthened his mental shield. The presence withdrew, but the evil taint lingered in his thoughts as he fumbled in his pocket for Kalesh's talisman.

'I don't think he's interested in stopping,' Leyoch said.

Varnia glanced up at Paddren trotting ahead on the trail, giving no thought to the clues his horse might be destroying. She cursed under her breath. 'We may as well follow him,' she said, moving back to where Leyoch had dismounted.

As she took the reins and hooked her right foot into the stirrup, a cry rang through the silent forest. The stallion reared and yanked the strap from her hand. She stumbled away from its flailing hooves and ran to Paddren.

'What's wrong?'

He gazed down at her, a wild look in his eyes. 'Kalesh is being attacked!'

Without warning, he sped away.

'What's happening?' Leyoch drew level and hoisted her up onto the horse behind him.

'It's Kalesh, he's being attacked.' She clung to Leyoch as he spurred Shadow after the wizard.

They trailed behind him, losing ground to the lighter horse until Paddren's momentum faltered and he slumped over the neck of his mount. They closed the gap and Leyoch snatched up the trailing reins as the mare tried to sidestep.

'Easy girl,' Leyoch said in a soothing tone. The mare responded to his familiar scent, allowing Varnia to check on Paddren. He seemed about to fall, so she grabbed a handful of his cloak to steady him. He groaned and made a feeble effort to move. She helped him sit up and her eyes widened as she saw a thin trickle of blood seep from his nose. 'Are you all right?'

He stared at her, dazed.

'What's going on, Paddren?' Leyoch demanded as his hand dropped to cover his sword.

Varnia grasped her knife and scanned the trees hemming them in on both sides.

'Kalesh just repelled me,' Paddren said. He drew the sword strapped to his saddlebags, the blade glinting in the sunlight.

'But I'll do whatever it takes to help him.'

VISIONS OF ZARUA

BOOK BLURB

Two wizards, 350 years apart. Can they save the realm of Paltria from Zarua's dark past?

An ancient darkness haunts the realm of Paltria. Apprentice wizard Paddren is plagued by visions of a city on the brink of annihilation. When his master dies in mysterious circumstances, the Royal Order of Wizards refuses to investigate.

Helped by his childhood friend, the skilled tracker Varnia, and her lover Leyoch, Paddren vows to find the killer.

The investigation leads Paddren down a sinister path of assassins, secret sects and creatures conjured by blood magic. But he is guided by a connection with a wizard from centuries ago - a wizard whose history holds the key to the horror at the heart of the abandoned city of Zarua. Can Paddren decipher his visions and save the Paltrian people before the dark menace of Zarua's past is unleashed?

Available in eBook, Paperback or audiobook from Amazon. It's also free to read on Kindle Unlimited.

PRAISE FOR VISIONS OF ZARUA

'…Visions of Zarua is very much a mystery stroke who dunit kind of a read, that just happens to be set in a mythical fantasy world with Wizards. But the two genres blend so beautifully together. This book really is an exquisite slow burner of a read, that needs to be savoured, there is no rushing this novel. Sit back, relax and enjoy the ride.' **Amazon Reviewer**

'Intriguing characters, strong structure, high stakes, memorable world. The Visions of Zarua packs a punch in delivering all of these. A superb story that fantasy readers will definitely enjoy!' **Amazon Reviewer**

'VISIONS OF ZARUA casts a shadow of excitement giving the fantasy genre a nice little jolt. Teeming with suspicion, lies, murder, and lurking darkness this book continues to twist building itself into a fierce storm that absorbs time and thrills its readers as the characters embark on a ruthless hunt for truth and sorcery.' **Amazon Reviewer**

GARRICK THE PROTECTOR

Their horse flew across the open ground, tearing up clods of earth to leave a trail no fool could miss. Garrick urged the horse on, his aunt's words ringing in his ears. He had to get Mara to Turrak before the guards learnt her secret and came for her.

'Come on.' He nudged his heels into the horse's sides and shook the reins.

Mara clung to him. She didn't speak, but her fear transferred through her vice-like grip; she was terrified of what the Assembly would do if they caught her. Stories of torture flashed through his head, but he brushed them aside as they ploughed along the path. Mara deserved a chance to live a normal life, but the Assembly would never allow that if they discovered her powers.

'Hold on,' he called back and heard Mara's muffled response as her arms wrapped tighter around his waist.

They ducked into a stand of trees and followed the narrow track. The woodland gave a brief reprieve from the blinding sun but soon the trees grew sparse, and the path widened out into open fields and hills. He stopped on the rise of a hill and gazed back in the direction of home but saw no sign of pursuit.

'We should've stopped to rest when there was cover,' Mara said as they headed downhill.

'I want to put more miles between us.' He stroked the mare's long neck, praying she could carry them a little further.

'She'll need to rest soon.'

'I know, don't worry.'

'Thank you, Garrick.' Mara's voice broke.

He nodded; glad she couldn't see his face. He was just as scared as she was.

Night was drawing in when they stopped in the trees at the top of a ridge. Smoke rose from a town far below, which he ignored and made a cold camp.

'Are you sure about this?'

He shot Mara a brazen smile. 'We need to rest somewhere and it's better to stay away from towns and villages when we can.'

She didn't look convinced as she stood by the horse and clutched the reins.

Garrick prised the leather straps away from her and led her to the blankets he'd spread out in the gap between two trees. 'Rest. You're exhausted.'

She stumbled away and sat hugging her knees to her chest. 'I've never slept outside before.'

Garrick grinned as he rubbed down the horse.

'It's not funny.' Mara hid a yawn behind her hand. 'Are we going to be safe here?'

'I'm sure the horse will warn us of any problems. And I can keep watch, I'm a light sleeper.'

Mara laughed. 'I've heard your snoring through the walls.' She cuddled her knees while he finished feeding the horse before spreading a blanket across its back.

'Try to focus on the new life waiting for you in Turrak. Your father always talked about how different things were there.'

'I miss him.'

Garrick slumped next to her. He had no words and they remained silent listening to echoes of the nocturnal forest waking around them. He heard shuffling in the undergrowth and the hoot of an owl, comforting sounds confirming their only companions were the creatures of the night.

'Garrick, why aren't you scared of magic like other people?'

He thought about the question as he stared into the trees. 'The way Uncle Bal explained it made it impossible to be scared. Magic is all around us, like nature. How can I fear nature? It's a part of life. It's like being afraid of life itself.' He shrugged. 'Sorry, that sounds stupid.'

'It's not stupid.' Mara rested her head against his shoulder. 'I feel safe with you, even out here when everyone is scared of people like me... of what I am.'

'You're still a person. A special person with the ability to help others. If they can't accept you, they don't deserve you.' He put his arm around her tiny shoulders. How could people fear such a kind, sweet girl?

She sniffed and he heard a muffled sob in the darkness.

A few days ago she'd been a normal farmer's daughter, now she was an exile, forced to leave behind everything and everyone she loved. It wasn't fair.

'I don't believe the ignorance of this society.' Anger swelled inside him as he pictured the mob gathered in the town square demanding the arrest of every known mystic. It wouldn't have been long before they came for Mara. They'd have sent her to Newington for the Assembly to deal with.

'Everything will be alright when we get to Turrak, won't it Garrick?'

'Of course it will.' He tried to stay calm for Mara's sake and drew up an image of her father. 'Uncle Bal said everyone is accepted in Turrak, with or without magic.'

'It will be exciting to visit the mountains at last.'

'Then we should get some rest, we still have a long way to travel.'

Garrick shifted position so Mara could lie down. He leant against a tree and studied the silent forest, though he couldn't pick out much in the dark.

'Thank you for helping me,' Mara muttered sleepily.

Garrick didn't relax until he heard the even breathing of her sleeping. He touched the dagger at his hip. Keeping Mara safe was all that mattered.

***

Garrick awoke with the dawn, his back stiff from sleeping propped against the tree. He stretched and then raided one of the supply bags his aunt had thrown together. As he fished out a loaf of flat bread, homesickness struck. Just yesterday they'd gathered around the table eating bread with honey and freshly churned butter.

He missed Mara's bickering brothers and his aunt's gentle smile. Garrick had moved in when Uncle Bal got too sick to work the farm and he'd taken over the tasks his cousins were too young to handle. There had never been an official agreement, he helped because they needed him. His own family were only across the valley and he regretted not having the chance to say goodbye.

'Morning,' Mara said as he handed her a portion of bread and the water skin.

He spotted the sweet pastries wrapped in cloth at the bottom of the bag. As agonising as it was to resist, he decided to save the treat for when Mara needed a reminder of home.

They ate the day-old bread and packed up the camp together.

As he led the mare to the edge of the forest, Garrick saw his mistake in selecting their night-time sanctuary. A group of woodsmen were heading towards the trees from the town. The men carried axes and led two horses with heavy chains attached to harnesses.

'We should take a different route.' He turned the mare's head and Mara followed him without question.

He led the horse deeper into the woods and soon lost all sense of direction. 'I hope this is still south,' he said under his breath; they had limited supplies and couldn't afford to be set off course.

Panic built in his chest as he thought of Mara's survival being reliant on him. He squared his shoulders and took a breath, clearing his mind the way his uncle had shown him. The change in his perception was instantaneous; the world filtered in and all panic subsided. He'd once asked Bal if it was magic. His uncle had laughed. 'You're learning to use your mind Garrick, there's nothing magical about it. But you do have a magic of your own – your heart is filled with selfless love. Few men can boast that, let alone a fourteen-year-old boy.'

That had been last year, just as Bal started showing signs of sickness and long before Mara's powers developed. Maybe if they'd manifested earlier, she could have saved her father. He barred the cynical thought, knowing Mara tortured herself with such notions every day.

As they emerged from the woods he checked the direction of the sun, relieved they were still on course. They mounted the horse and continued their journey. They were soon rewarded with a sighting of the Turrak Mountains, the peaks rising majestically in the distance. Garrick swallowed his relief; they still had a long way to go.

***

'A few more miles and we'll be safe,' he said twisting in the saddle to face Mara. 'The Assembly won't bother to hunt you this far south.'

'I hope that's true.'

They'd travelled three days and managed to avoid all settlements, but their supplies were almost gone and the grain for the horse would soon run out. They walked the mare for a while, allowing her a break while they stretched their legs and snacked on the edible berries they found growing in the understory of the forest. It was pitiful fare, making do with what little the creatures had left behind. The sour berries did more to start his hunger than quell it.

His belly rumbled so he focused on his surroundings. The air smelt woody and wild, the greens of the leaves filling his vision with vibrant colour. He closed his eyes and listened to the distant tweet of a bird and the gentle brush of wind through the leaves. 'Kalaya is filled with beauty. I never appreciated how special it was before.'

'My brothers would tease you if they heard you talking like that.'

He squared his shoulders. 'I'm not afraid of what people think of me.'

'I don't think you're afraid of anything,' Mara said seriously.

He let the comment pass. Mara needed him to be strong, so he'd be her protector on this journey and for as long as she needed him.

They stopped by a stream and snacked on the last of their supplies while the horse drank her fill. The babble of water rushing downstream over the shallow bed of stones seemed as though nature played her tranquil music just for them.

'This reminds me of how your father used to talk about travelling Kalaya before settling on the farm.'

Mara's gaze looked faraway. 'Father always told such wonderful tales. We'd even talked of visiting Turrak together one day. It's sad he never had the chance.'

The horse stopped feeding on the juicy grass. Her head snapped up, ears twitching as she snorted in alarm.

Garrick waved Mara to silence as he picked out the distinctive sound of other travellers heading their way.

They mounted and prepared to flee, but a group of five riders appeared from the forest before they could get away. The men headed for the stream but pulled up on the reins at the sight of company. They wore black masks across their faces, all with differing degrees of coverage. The effect implied they were handmade rather than part of a standard uniform. He'd heard rumours of masked riders attacking Kalayan people, but that had been the last thing on his mind when fleeing their home.

One rider nudged his horse forward from the group. 'Nice mount. Hand her over along with your belongings.'

'I don't think so.' Garrick sat tall in the saddle. His fingers flexed, ready to grab the hunting dagger at his side. 'We may not have much, but what we do have is ours.'

The leader sneered, his piercing brown eyes showing through slits in the fabric of his mask. 'Maybe you didn't hear me correctly, boy. I said hand over the horse, and we'll let you live.'

Mara tensed, but Garrick remained calm. 'Make me.'

The rider laughed. 'It will be a pleasure. Then we get the girl and the horse.'

Garrick shook his head. 'I have another proposition. Let your mounts take a drink before you turn back the way you came. No one needs to get hurt.'

'You, against five of us?' The leader laughed and his men echoed it. 'It's time we taught you a lesson, boy. Show you what playing the hero gets you.'

'Take the horse and flee while I distract them,' he hissed as he slipped from the saddle.

'No,' Mara said as he walked away.

He swore but didn't look back, focusing instead on the riders.

The lead horseman dismounted and pulled his sword free with a flourish. The weapon was long, its sharp blade glinting. He grinned as he threw the weapon from hand to hand, chuckling at the size of the simple hunting knife Garrick brandished.

His opponent advanced, striding forward with a confidence Garrick tried to match as he drew the battle away from Mara.

They circled one another.

'Go on Trey, teach him a lesson.' The other horsemen cat-called and urged the masked warrior on.

Garrick breathed slowly and used the technique his uncle had taught him to clear his thoughts. He concentrated on his adversary, studying the man's every move, judging how he stood as he swung the blade. Trey favoured his right side as he postured and showed off his skills.

Garrick stood steady, waiting. Trey grew bored and challenged him, making the first strike. His blade clashed against Garrick's dagger, sending shock waves through his arms.

The masked man's movements were smooth and controlled; he intended to toy with his victim and entertain his friends.

When he lunged again, Garrick ducked to the left. Avoiding the sword as it flashed past him, he swiped out with his dagger. The blade caught his opponent across his unprotected side as they passed each other.

Always keep your knife sharp. Uncle Bal's voice echoed in his head. *Despatch your prey with dignity and mercy. Limit its suffering by making the kill swift.*

The masked man stumbled away while his friends cheered him on. 'Come on. He's yours, Trey.'

Trey turned and raised the blade, but his arm dropped to his side and the weapon slipped from his fingers. He frowned in confusion when he touched his torso and his fingers came away bloody. The rider dropped to his knees and fell face first in the dirt.

Silence reigned in the clearing.

Garrick stepped forward and picked up the fallen sword. He swung the weapon, judging its quality and weight. It was heavier than the practice swords he'd used with his brothers, but less cumbersome than the axe he used to make firewood.

He rolled his shoulders and formed a fighting stance as he faced the four remaining men. 'Who's next?'

A rider roared and charged his horse at Garrick.

He waited, poised on the balls of his feet, and dived out of the way as the horse rushed him.

The sword sailed over his head. The horseman swerved and turned, charging again.

Trapped with thick bushes to his right and the horseman bearing down on his left, Garrick stood firm and raised his sword. He saw the whites of his opponent's eyes as he galloped in for the kill.

Their blades clashed and the weapon was torn from his hand, jarring his shoulder. As the horseman's momentum carried him forward, Garrick spotted another rider going for Mara.

Garrick threw his hunting dagger. It spun through the air and embedded to the hilt in the rider's back. He toppled to the ground as his horse reared. Neighing, it bolted into the trees.

The other horses jerked sideways to follow as herd instinct kicked in. The three remaining men fought their mounts for control. Once tamed, they dismounted and formed a line facing Garrick.

He whipped up the sword from where it had fallen in the dirt and eyed his adversaries. He'd been lucky so far, but the odds were still not in his favour.

They circled him and charged. He blocked strike after strike, only able to retreat. He took several cuts from glancing blows until miscommunication between two of the men saw them lunge together and wrong foot each other. Garrick stabbed in the opening, taking out an opponent with a savage cut to his thigh. He rolled on the ground wailing as he clutched the wounded leg, all attempts at menace forgotten.

Three men dead or incapacitated, but Garrick was still standing.

'My offer remains,' he said, breathing hard. His heart raced but his hand was steady, the bloodied sword pointing at the masked men. 'We don't have anything worth stealing, certainly nothing worth dying for.'

The two men looked from their whimpering comrade to each other, and for the first time Garrick realised they were hardly older than himself.

He lowered the tip of the blade and took a step back but kept the fighter's stance ready to spring into attack.

They hesitated before grabbing their injured friend and retreating to where the horses waited by the stream.

Garrick watched them flee into the trees and listened until the sound of their flight faded to nothing. He tossed the sword at his feet and sneered in disgust at the two corpses in the clearing. His first kills.

'We should take their weapons.' His voice was gruff as he scanned the forest. 'They might come back.'

Mara slid from the saddle. 'I doubt it. You were terrifying.'

He clenched shaking hands into fists as the magnitude of what he'd done sunk in.

She joined him and patted his tensed shoulder. 'You did what you had to cousin. They would've killed us.'

Garrick nodded, unconvinced. Why was the world full of bloodthirsty men out to take what wasn't theirs?

He unstrapped the sword belt from the man they'd called Trey and attached it to his own waist. While Mara followed suit with the other rider's belt, he scrabbled in the dirt for the lost sword and searched the bodies for hidden daggers.

'Shame they took the spare horse,' he muttered staring at their own mount as she cropped the grass.

The mare looked thin and tired; he didn't know how much longer she could carry them both.

He winced as he stood, his chest burning. The fabric of his shirt was torn though he didn't recall the blow that caused it; a couple of nicks on the arms were all he remembered in the heat of the battle.

Mara's eyes widened at the blood sticking his shirt to his body. 'You're wounded. Let me heal you.'

'Later,' he said. 'I need to get you safe.' He stumbled as he reached their horse but couldn't find the strength to mount the beast.

Mara rushed to his side and made him sit. 'It's your turn to let me help you.'

She peeled open his shirt to reveal a long slash across his torso. Mara wet a cloth in the stream and bathed the skin clean of blood. 'It's only a flesh wound, but it will keep bleeding if you try to ride.'

'Go on then.' He gritted his teeth, unsure what to expect.

When Mara put her hand to his body, warmth grew around the wound. His chest itched as the flesh sealed together. The skin puckered tight, forming an angry scar.

Mara went pale and he pulled away from her. 'Enough.'

She fell back, spent, and took a moment to catch her breath. 'Sorry it looks awful. This is all so new to me.'

He traced a finger over the red, raised flesh. 'My first battle scar.' Garrick swamped Mara in a hug. 'Thank you, little cousin.'

She pulled away and hit him on the arm. 'Enough with the little, we're practically the same age.'

Grinning, they helped each other to stand. He gave her a boost into the saddle before taking a last glance at the bodies of the two men he'd killed. Mara had removed their masks and laid their limp hands across their chests in the death pose. They looked like normal men, no trace of the would-be murderers they'd been in life.

'Over a horse...' Shaking his head, Garrick rubbed the mare's side. Then he mounted up and flicked the reins, leading them into the forest.

***

The next day, as they crossed through a succession of empty fields, riders appeared from a corridor of trees ahead of them. Garrick cursed, there was no safe retreat and no way to outrun them across the open ground. Turrak loomed in front of them; they'd come so close.

Garrick drew the mare to a stop and could almost hear her snort in relief as he slid from the saddle. He contemplated smacking her rump and sending Mara off alone, but one look at his cousin's defiant expression stayed his hand.

She dismounted and they both unsheathed their swords and faced the riders. He stole another glance at her.

'At least we tried,' Mara said.

'It's not over yet, cousin.' He rolled his shoulders, working out the tension in his bunched muscles. They ached after the blows he'd deflected yesterday but Mara had healed the other wounds last night.

'I'm not giving up this adventure without a fight.' Garrick brandished his weapon at the riders. These ones wore neither masks, nor the blue of the Assembly, but they were still a threat to Mara.

The horsemen drew to a halt a good distance away. One of them, a golden-haired warrior, walked his horse forward from the group and held up empty hands. 'We have no intention of fighting you.'

'I won't let you hurt her. You'll have to come through me.'

'We don't want to hurt anyone.'

'The last men that tried to attack us won't be bothering anyone again.'

'We won't hurt her, Garrick. I promise you.'

He stood firm, unmoved by the words of the stranger. 'How do you know my name?'

The tall warrior smiled. His expression was friendly as he dismounted and walked towards them. He flung his cloak over his shoulder showing no weapons hung from his waist. There were no weapons Garrick could see, though he reasoned this man could be just as deadly without them.

'The Sentinel sent us to find you. We've come to escort Mara to Turrak.'

Garrick and Mara turned to each other and slowly lowered their swords.

The Turrak Mountains reared behind the warrior. Could they really be safe? Garrick wished he had his uncle's instincts about people. He stared at each of the strangers trying to judge their hearts. 'I'll stay with Mara until I'm sure she's safe.'

'I expected nothing less. You're welcome to stay with us as long as you please.' The tall warrior held out his hand. 'I'm Hafender. Welcome to the exiles.'

They travelled with the team of six exiles and as the day wore on without incident, Garrick began to relax though he still bore the responsibility for Mara's safety on his wide shoulders.

His cousin seemed at ease amongst the strangers. She'd taken a shine to Rike, one of the younger mystics under Hafender's command. Rike spoke openly to Mara, and his simple approach seemed to help her accept her new status as an exile. He'd also promised to help her learn to use her new skills when they reached Turrak.

Garrick stroked the raised flesh of the scar under his shirt; with the right training who knew how proficient she could become at healing. Uncle Bal would be so proud.

Mara laughed and joked with their new companions, glowing in the company of other mystics.

The exiles shared their supplies. After days of near starvation, Garrick devoured the cheese with a tangy fruit preserve and chewy bread that didn't threaten to snap his teeth. He washed it down with the sweetest apple cider he'd ever tasted. 'I could get used to this.'

'There's plenty more where that came from.' Hafender laughed heartily.

'You might regret saying that. Back home Garrick's appetite is legendary.' A hint of sadness flashed in Mara's eyes, her words reminding them of what they'd left behind.

'I think our supplies can cope,' Hafender said, winking at Mara.

A few hours later they reached the foot of the mountains and were greeted by watchmen dressed in grey to match the stone pass they guarded.

The men saluted Hafender and waved their small party through. Garrick gaped in awe as they travelled up the long pass that cut through the imposing Turrak mountain range. It was a tough journey, but the excitement of their guides rubbed off and made Garrick pulse race with anticipation. Somehow it felt like they were coming home.

Their group stopped at the top of the ridge. Mara and Garrick stood side by side soaking in the view of the valley opening out beneath them. Peace enveloped him, seeping through his veins and into his core.

Mara grinned through her tears and hugged him tight, shocking him with the strength of her embrace. 'I finally feel as though I belong somewhere. Thank you for helping me.'

Garrick slung his arm around her shoulders, dwarfing her slight frame. Together they gazed into the valley and the idyllic life of the exiles. No blue-clad Assemblymen, filled with their own superiority, strutted the streets. No town guards lurked in the shadows waiting to arrest anyone for showing the slightest sign of being different. There were just Kalayan people going about their everyday lives without fear of judgement.

'Uncle Bal was right; you will be happy here. I'm glad I had the chance to see the magic of Kalaya; I won't ever forget this moment.'

She slugged him playfully in the stomach, catching him off guard and reminding him of her upbringing with boisterous younger brothers. 'Don't go getting all sentimental on me, cousin.'

He laughed, heartened to see the old Mara emerge from the self-imposed prison she'd retreated into since discovering her powers.

Hafender joined them, smiling brightly. 'The Sentinel welcomes you both to our home. He wants you to know you will always have a place here amongst us.'

Garrick studied the stone houses mirroring the mountains surrounding them. There were also fields of crops, livestock, and horses. A lake glistened in the low sunshine and an orchard spread across the valley. People and nature were coexisting and Kalaya's magic was a part of it all. He felt it pull at him, shaping his destiny.

A group of women approached Mara. With a reassuring nod from Hafender they led her away.

Garrick stood beside the tall mystic, fighting the urge to follow.

Hafender smiled. 'Don't worry, Mara is safe in Turrak. She'll thrive here.'

Garrick had no doubt this haven from the Assembly was where Mara needed to be. 'I wish her father could see her so happy.'

'He can.' Hafender waved his arms wide. 'He's a part of the magic now.'

Garrick pictured Uncle Bal when he was strong and healthy. He remembered the spark of knowing in his eyes, the hint that he was at one with their magical island home. He sensed Bal's love surround him, guiding his path.

'What about you, Garrick? What are your plans?'

He eyed the exiles' domain. 'I'll stick around Turrak for a few days, just to make sure Mara settles in.'

Hafender grinned and slapped him on the back. 'That's good to hear. Come on, I'll give you a guided tour.'

***

This story features characters from Silent Sea Chronicles and is set ten years before book 1 - The Lost Sentinel. Read on for an excerpt.

THE LOST SENTINEL
EXCERPT CHAPTER TWO

Tei opened her eyes to the cold morning air and shivered into her cloak. The fluty song of a robin broke the ethereal silence and she sucked in a breath, hardly able to believe they'd made it through the night. She forced herself to stand, though it was an effort to leave the warmth of her father's side. He slept peacefully, so she left him cocooned in her cloak and blankets. Huddling her arms around her shivering body, she ducked into the trees to scout the hilltop for food.

She slunk through the frostbitten leaves littering the ground, cautious of every sound. Her skin crawled with fear and she jumped at the slightest breeze, imagining beasts or mystics stalking her through the shady woods.

The harsh autumn frosts had stripped the land of edible fare; all she found was a patch of rotting mushrooms. Tei turned to head back to her father, but she caught a glimpse of the sunrise through the bare branches of an oak tree. She inched her way forward and watched the rising sun bathe the landscape below in golden light. As her father had predicted, it was a beautiful morning, and she hoped fervently it would prove a better day than the last.

Movement below caught her eye and she merged back amongst the trees, hoping the two men in the distance hadn't spotted her. Her heart pounded as she dashed back to her father's side. 'Father…'

His eyes flickered open and he squinted as he focused on her face.

'Father, there are two men heading this way.'

'I can sense them,' he said, grimacing as he struggled to sit.

Tei helped him get comfortable and then passed him the water skin. She watched him sip while she tugged at a loose thread on her tunic.

'Don't worry, Tei. They're exiles like us; they're coming to help.'

She sighed and reached for her pack, searching through the supplies to see what was left of their rations - a few oatcakes and the apples she'd managed to forage the previous day.

'Why don't you eat something?' She offered her father half the meagre breakfast.

Wrinkling his nose, he pulled the blankets up to his chin. 'You go ahead.'

Tei crunched on an apple as she scanned behind them. There was no sign of pursuit on their back trail, but memories of yesterday's attack haunted her.

As she glanced across at her father, the last bite of apple turned sour in her mouth. He looked so frail; she doubted he'd be fit to travel for days.

Aching with hunger and tortured by worry, Tei packed away the rest of the food to stall temptation and sipped on water to dull the ache in her belly. Inevitably, her gaze returned to her father.

'I know you're watching me,' he said, without opening his eyes.

The arrival of the men saved her from replying. They hiked up the slope into view and trampled along the leaf-strewn path towards Tei and her father. The first man was tall and heavyset with bulging muscles and a baldpate, though he could only have been in his twenties. The second man was leaner and a little older, and wore a look of intensity - heightened by his guarded expression. She felt the presence of island magic smouldering inside him.

Tei's stomach constricted and she swallowed hard as the men stopped a few feet away. Swords hung from their waists and they both wore bows slung across their backs. Her hand twitched, wanting to draw her dagger, but she held her breath and glanced across at her father.

He grinned at the new arrivals. 'Rike, come over here.'

'Migil,' the older of the two men said, stepping forward and crouching in front of her father.

As he pulled Rike into a bear hug, Tei saw a glimmer of tears in her father's eyes. 'It's good to see you again.' He patted Rike's back, grimacing with the small movement. 'So grown up... you were just a lad when I left Turrak.'

'It's been a long time, nearly twenty years.' Rike pulled away from the embrace and his face finally relaxed into a smile.

'Too long...' her father trailed off.

Tei felt ill at ease in the silence, imagining the life her father would have led if he'd stayed in the mountains.

'This is Garrick.' Rike indicated his companion.

'It's good to finally meet the legend in the flesh,' Garrick said, smiling warmly as he shook her father's hand.

'And it's a pleasure to meet you. I've heard impressive tales about you, my young friend.'

Garrick laughed and looked bashful.

Tei wondered why these strangers regarded her father with such admiration.

Her father caught her gaze and winked. 'This is my delightful daughter, Tei. Tei, meet Rike and Garrick; two finer men I'm sure you'll never meet.'

'I'll take that compliment. Nice to meet you.' Garrick thrust his huge hand towards her.

His skin was callused against hers, yet his grip was surprisingly gentle and his blue eyes sparkled with friendliness as he looked down at her.

'Hello,' she said, at a loss for anything else to say.

Rike stepped forward, nodding a greeting as she took his out-stretched hand. She tried to smile in return, but the anguish betrayed in his eyes caught her off-guard.

'Thank you for coming to our aid,' her father said.

'I wish we'd arrived sooner.' Rike looked at the ground.

'The attack was… unexpected.' Her father paused, struggling to catch his breath. 'The boy was… foolhardy…' His words dissolved into a cough.

Tei waited for the coughing fit to pass before offering him some water. 'Are you alright?'

He nodded, though his face was drained of colour and he looked gaunt in the early morning sunshine. Forcing down a few sips from the water skin, he attempted to clear his throat but the breath rattled in his chest.

'The boy's defeat has given us a short period of grace, we have time to rest and…' Rike began, but her father waved him to silence.

'We can't afford to be complacent,' he said, wheezing.

'We saw no sign of Masked Riders on our travels, but we all know they're a canny bunch,' Garrick said.

'Masked Riders?' Tei looked around the small group, waiting for someone to enlighten her.

Her father opened his mouth as if to speak but his breathing became shallow and rasping. He slumped against the wall, clutching his chest.

Tei dropped the water skin and turned to Rike. 'Do something. Help him.'

The mystic sat down and placed his hand against her father's forehead until his distressed look disappeared and he relaxed into sleep.

Tei felt a gentle tap on her shoulder, urging her to stand. She stood and turned to look up at Garrick.

'Let's give them some space. Rike knows wounds; he'll do what he can to help your father.'

'But I want to stay with him.'

Garrick eyes softened with understanding. 'I know, just give them a few minutes. We can gather some wood for a fire.'

She saw Garrick exchange a look with Rike over her shoulder, before the big man led her away. Reluctantly, Tei allowed him to steer her towards the eastern slope where the oak trees grew more abundantly. They collected sticks and kindling on their descent and Garrick only permitted them to stop when her father was out of sight. He took the sticks from her trembling hands and settled down against the base of a large oak tree.

Tei selected an old oak a few paces away from Garrick and sank back against the knobbly bark, feeling its roughness through her clothing. She closed her eyes and focused on the tree and the many organisms living within it. Then she attuned her senses further afield, tapping into the magic of nature surrounding her on the hillside. She chased after the meditative state to quell her nerves, but nothing happened. She dug her fingers into the earth and drew recklessly on her connection with the island. Kalaya was waiting. It channelled through her veins, welcoming her with its embrace. Tei longed to delve deeper and explore more of the island's magic, but reluctantly she pulled back, exercising the same caution that had ruled her life in Seatown.

An image of her father's pain-contorted face flashed in her mind. She glanced up the ridge, wondering if Rike had finished treating his wounds. As she turned back, she caught Garrick studying her.

'Sorry,' he said and returned his attention to sorting through the woodpile.

She watched him deftly snap the branches into uniform size, discarding any damp sticks as he came across them. A tidy pile was building at his side, but eventually he looked up at her.

'Rike's a talented mystic. Your father's in good hands.'

'What's this about, Garrick?'

He shrugged and turned away.

'My father's told me nothing. I don't even know why we were attacked.'

'Neither do I.' Garrick's muscled shoulders tensed. 'All I know is that your father contacted Rike, saying he'd been warned you were in danger.'

'Danger from what?' She held his gaze, waiting out the awkward silence hanging between them.

'I'm just a protector; I don't get involved in the ways of mystics.'

'What about these Masked Riders you mentioned? Who are they?'

'It's a stupid nickname. We know very little about them or their motives for attacking our people. Some say they are searching for...' His deep voice filtered into nothing and he looked away, embarrassed.

Tei recalled the young mystic's words to her father. *'Hand over the girl...'*

She stood up abruptly, brushing the leaves from her clothes as though the act could brush aside the disturbing thoughts forming in her mind.

'I think it's time I found out what's really going on.' Without waiting for his response, Tei marched up the steep slope.

She heard Garrick jogging to catch her up and glanced across at him, seeing him clutching the hastily retrieved pile of firewood in his arms.

As they crested the rise, she saw her father was still propped against the wall, sleeping. Rike sat close by, his head bowed as if deep in thought. He glanced up at their arrival and rose to intercept them.

'I can't help him; I'm sorry.' He drew level with her and as she looked into his grief-stricken eyes, Tei felt her world fall apart.

'He said it was a few cracked ribs…'

Rike shook his head. 'He has internal injuries bleeding inside, poisoning his blood. His magic has held it at bay up to now, but his strength is failing.'

Rike reached out and squeezed her shoulders. She pushed him away, glaring at him through her tears. 'Go away, leave us be…'

She saw the wounded look in Rike's eyes, but Garrick pulled him away before he could protest.

Her father stirred and Tei dropped to her knees by his side, the two men forgotten.

'Tei…'

'Why didn't you tell me how badly you were hurt?'

'I'm sorry.' His words dissolved into a fit of coughing and she winced at the pain etched across his brow.

'Tei, I…' Another cough racked through him and specks of blood flecked his lips as he struggled to catch his breath.

'Don't try to speak.' She fumbled with the water skin and held it to his mouth.

He shook his head. 'I have to tell you something. Something I should have told you a long time ago.' He reached for her hand as he sucked in a shaky breath. 'Tei, I'm not your father.'

The Lost Sentinel
Book Blurb

The magical island of Kalaya is dying. Only Tei, an exiled mystic, can save it.

The Assembly controls Kalaya. Originally set up to govern, they now persecute those with magic and exile them to the Turrak Mountains. Tei, a tailor's daughter, has always hidden her magic but when her father's old friend visits and warns them to flee to the mountains she must leave her old life behind.

On the journey, an attack leaves her father mortally wounded. He entrusts her into the care of two exiles, Rike and Garrick, and on his deathbed makes a shocking confession.

Tei joins the exiles search for their new Sentinel - the only person capable of restoring the fading magic. But mysterious Masked Riders are hunting the Sentinel too, and time, as well as hope, is running out.

Against mounting odds it will take friendship, heartache and sacrifice to succeed, but is Tei willing to risk everything she loves to save the island magic?

Available from Amazon in ebook, paperback and audiobook format. Also available as a trilogy box set and free to read on Kindle Unlimited.

Praise for the Silent Sea Chronicles

'...this story bowled me over, it was an absolutely outstanding epic fantasy and the kind of writing fantasy authors should be aspiring to.' **Amazon Reviewer**

'...Suzanne Rogerson can certainly make you forget time... A super start to what is going to be a sensational story, just make sure you are part of it from the beginning' **Amazon Vine Voice Reviewer.**

'THE LOST SENTINEL contains plenty of action, intrigue, and challenges throughout, making this a thrilling fantasy adventure... it whisked me away to someplace magical, alluring, and dangerous.' **Amazon reviewer**.

'A story in which the authors world building is exceptional, I was immersed in Tei's story from beginning to end and the characters were fantastically developed.' **Amazon Vine Voice Reviewer.**

'With all the intricate world building, interesting characters and epic journey they all partake in, this book had me glued to it from the first page. As soon as I finished it, I was making a grab for book two to see what happened next! Suzanne Rogerson has written a fantastic start to this series - I love her writing style, and that she doesn't shy away from putting her characters through some tough challenges as the story progresses.' **Amazon Vine Voice Reviewer.**

WAR WOUNDS

The attacker slid off Calder's blade and died on the sand at his feet. Calder glowered at the body; his emotions numb. Slowly sound filtered in. Not the clash of blades and battle cries, but the eerie echoes of the dying reverberating in his head.

He scanned the length of the beach. No one else was fighting; the enemy were dead. They'd captured two boats and pulled them up onto the shore. The boats crackled and burned sending black smoke into the air. His fellow soldiers were patting each other on the back but it didn't feel like victory to Calder.

Putting away his bloodied weapon, he wiped his hands on his breeches wanting to be cleansed of the deaths he'd caused. Protecting his homeland was one thing, but today he'd witnessed mindless carnage.

As he stared at the bodies, the destroyed camp and the celebrating Cantayan soldiers his skin prickled in the familiar way; something was amiss. Striding through the makeshift troop of farmers and soldiers, Calder searched out his childhood friend Captain Ashan.

Offering a quick salute, he glanced around to ensure they wouldn't be overheard. 'This doesn't feel right Captain.'

'Calder, my friend, you're a craftsman. You're more used to working with a chisel or axe than a sword.'

'I'm hardly a craftsman, I've failed at everything I've turned my hand to.'

Ashan grinned. 'The point I'm making is you're not a soldier. I wouldn't expect you to be happy after battle.'

'This wasn't a battle; it was a slaughter.'

The captain's expression hardened. 'Your point?'

Calder ignored the harsh tone and spun around to indicate the burnt out remains of the long boats. 'Why did they travel here in force, only to splinter off into small raiding parties? They would have been stronger sticking together.'

Captain Ashan examined the battleground with a calculating look, casting his gaze across the downed enemy and the temporary camp they'd built by the shore.

'Take this position. They had little by way of defence and no line of retreat with the sea at their backs. They could never hold against us.'

The captain still refused to answer, scowling at the bodies of the raiders as though their corpses would reveal the answers.

'Ash, you can see what I'm saying, can't you? When the battle reached them here it was only ever going to end one way.'

His friend sighed. 'To be honest, I don't like it either.'

As they scanned the bodies, one of the raiders moved. They rushed over to him and Ashan kicked away the fallen weapon, a battered sword of inferior craftsmanship. Calder dropped to his knees and flipped the man onto his back.

The gaping wound in the man's stomach made his own contract in response. He would never survive such an injury without a healer. Calder's basic knowledge of wounds confirmed the man had little time left. He put pressure on the entry point and the man's eyes flew open as he groaned in pain.

Ashan stood above them looking from Calder to the enemy.

'What's your purpose in Cantaya?' The captain leant down, his unsheathed dagger glinting in the sun.

'To conquer,' the man spat.

The captain waved his arm to encompass the fallen raiders and the celebrating Cantayan men. 'Looks to me like you've done a terrible job.'

The dying man sneered, showing no fear.

'Why are you really here?'

'To conquer you.'

The captain crouched lower and studied the foreigner's face. 'You're lying.' He pushed Calder's hand away and the blood flowed freely. The man groaned, his only show of weakness.

'Last chance. Why are you here?'

He laughed in response, but it turned into a scream as the captain stuck his fingers in the wound. 'State your purpose here.'

The two of them locked gazes.

Ashan pressed his dagger to the man's throat. 'Why did you land in Cantaya? What are you after?' His barrage of questions continued.

The man smiled a bloody smile. He spat blood in the captain's face and then leant into the sharpened steel. It pierced his flesh, spraying them with arterial blood.

Calder tried to staunch the flow as the captain watched on, the next question dying on his lips.

Ashan glared at their prisoner long after he was dead and only stirred when Calder closed the man's unseeing eyes.

'I think he was telling the truth,' Calder said, comprehension making him shiver.

Captain Ashan swore under his breath before shouting at the nearby soldiers who were too busy celebrating to realise something was wrong.

Calder surveyed the scene as the men stopped celebrating. Bodies of their own dead were pulled to one side. There were mercifully few Cantayan fatalities but many sported injuries.

'Check the enemy!' The captain barked. 'I want to question anyone found alive!'

The mood sobered as they followed orders and checked the two dozen bodies spread across the clearing. Calder joined in the search, his guts churning at the horrific injuries – so many unpleasant ways to die.

'Calder, to me.' The captain ordered as the only man found alive was dragged before him.

Calder examined him. He was barely conscious, bleeding out from his severed arm and other cuts to his torso. Blood loss had made him pale, and his skin was cold and clammy. The wound above his elbow joint was congealing but still leaked blood. Calder applied a tourniquet, though it was futile.

'He doesn't have long.' Calder gave the dying man a little water which revived him.

Licking pale lips, the man stared at Calder.

'Why did you invade our home?' Calder asked.

The man spoke but the language was incomprehensible, his voice scarcely above a whisper.

Captain Ashan tried to muscle in with his heavy-handed line of questioning and his bloody dagger drawn.

Calder waved him back, holding the gaze of the dying man. 'Why are you in Cantaya?'

'…seeking…' was the only word Calder understood before the man convulsed and died in his arms.

Captain Ashan paced around them with a face like thunder. It unnerved the men to see their composed leader act so out of character and Calder shot him a warning look.

Ashan straightened his shoulders before facing his men. 'Build a fire. Let's burn these bastards.'

As the soldiers set to work, the captain's gaze came to rest on Calder. 'This was a diversion. All these raids are diverting us from their true purpose.'

'But what's that?'

'I don't know.' Ashan grabbed the nearest scout. 'Take the fastest horse we have and ride to the castle. Get word to the king. We've been duped.'

***

Calder trudged into the grounds of the castle alongside the other foot soldiers in his troop. Captain Ashan and his cavalrymen had set off at first light to report to the king directly, leaving the stragglers to catch up.

It had been two weeks since their shoreside victory and they'd received no word as to why the enemy were pillaging their way through Cantaya. They'd engaged with another raiding party but learnt nothing of use; no one talked even under the captain's interrogation. Before he left Ashan had confided his hopes that other patrols had had more success understanding the foreigners' intentions. There had been no sightings since, and all reports indicated the raiders had left as mysteriously as they arrived.

Before Calder could follow the rest of his squad to the barracks, an old soldier from the cavalry division accosted him.

'Captain Ashan says you should report to his office.' The old man reeled out directions and left Calder to find his own way.

He walked through the castle grounds seeing signs of the troubled times hitting the realm. The castle, where he'd briefly apprenticed as a stone mason, was packed with training soldiers. Before it had been a place of outward tranquillity and political prowess.

He found the officer's quarters in the new structure tacked onto the west wing of the castle. Captain Ashan was alone pacing, nervousness written in the lines on his face. Some of the childhood insecurities showed through the cracks in his demeanour, reminding Calder of the boy he grew up with rather than the tough captain he'd become.

Ashan nodded greeting. 'I saw the king this morning and he's confirmed our fears. Raiders have been attacking throughout the kingdom and into neighbouring Navatasa. We've seen them off, but the king has no plans to let the matter drop. He's enlisting his best tacticians to discover more about these raids.'

'I'm sure you can help. You're a fine strategist, Ashan.'

Ashan looked displeased, his voice dropping. 'He wants me to team up with the Navatasan delegates, but it's a fool's errand. We can trust the Navatasans as much as we can trust these damn raiders. We can't make peace with either of them. We have no idea of their agendas.'

'I'm sure the king is doing what he must to keep the peace.'

'It wouldn't surprise me if the Navatasans paid the raiders to terrorise us just to persuade the king to abdicate his throne.'

'That's a traitorous suggestion. We're allies.'

'That's what they want us to believe. It's common knowledge certain members of the monarchy want to reunite the broken realms and bring all under their control. But how would raiders know our history?'

'I don't know.'

'Because someone told them where we're vulnerable. Why else land here, and why now?'

Calder shrugged and Ashan resumed pacing. During the months of serving with him, Calder knew the repetitive motion helped his old friend gather his thoughts.

'At least the two realms joined forces and saw them off,' Calder said.

'No, we did that, the Cantayans! The Navatasans hardly bloodied their swords.'

Calder held his tongue; allowing his friend's deep-seated distrust of their neighbours to go unchallenged even if it did cloud his judgement.

'Now I'm supposed to play envoy to the bastards.'

'It might not be that bad.'

Ashan shook his head, looking distracted. 'It's not like the king to make such rash decisions, especially where his traitorous former family are involved. I suspect that witch has his ear,' he finished, his nostrils flaring.

'Witch?' There was no time to question him as the door opened and one of the king's servants stepped into the room requesting the captain's presence.

'See you back at the barracks, soldier,' Ashan said in parting.

Calder hurried away, hoping the dismissal would soon become more permanent. He thought of his wife waiting at home and smiled as he imagined her dimpled cheeks. He'd received no reply from his last letter home. Correspondence between them had been sporadic with the constantly changing locations. Now he had a horrible feeling he was about to be roped into the captain's new mission.

As Calder walked back through the grounds, he saw a woman slip out from a side door of the castle and duck along the shadows of the building. Something about her set his nerves tingling.

The woman stopped and turned back, trapping him with her gaze. A charge like a lightning bolt flooded his limbs.

She nodded acknowledgment before disappearing around the corner of the building.

Calder remained rooted to the spot. It was as though a flame had gone out inside him chilling him to the bone.

He memorised her face with its distinctively sharp nose and chin, and frame of raven black hair. She had an air of intensity about her which made her stand out from the other visitors to the castle.

Calder hurried to the barracks and dumped his pack on a free pallet bed. The other soldiers were already out on the training ground, but Captain Ashan had granted him a reprieve; a benefit of being friends with the captain though that favouritism didn't always go down well with his fellow soldiers.

Calder stripped off his coat and weapons and waited for news from the captain. Sounds of practice combat drifted in from the courtyard and he sighed, his arms aching at the idea of picking up a sword again.

He pictured Arliss. Would he finally be granted leave to see her?

The months apart felt like years, and he missed the simple life he'd enjoyed living on the outskirts of the village in his old family home. Though secluded, with Arliss for company it had never been lonely. His father's trade as a charcoal burner saw the need for such a remote home. Calder had inherited the cottage upon his death but not the inclination to continue the family craft. It was a dirty business that clogged his lungs and made it hard to breathe. Stone masonry had not been much better, and then there was his attempt at becoming a wheelwright by apprenticing with his father-in-law. Arliss had teased him about his failures before reeling off an extensive list of his redeeming qualities, punctuating each with a kiss. Her eyes would twinkle with mischief, dimples forming in her cheeks…

Ashan's arrival broke Calder from his memories.

His childhood friend was the son of the village blacksmith. Ashan's impressive sword skills had ensured his swift rise through the ranks of the king's army to become captain but now he looked exhausted by his role as he sank down on the opposite bed. 'The king has issued new orders.'

Calder tried to read his friend, but his closed expression gave away nothing.

'It's deemed the threat has passed. Those conscripted are to be released from service.'

'What does that mean?'

'It means you get to go home to your wife. I, however, still have a job to undertake.'

Calder's mood switched from elation to worry for his friend; they'd been through a lot in the last few months.

'What will you do?' Calder asked.

'I'm to continue investigating these raiders. I could have requested your service, but you have Arliss waiting for you. I wouldn't want to keep you apart longer than necessary.'

Calder gulped and held his tongue, duty tearing him in both directions.

Ashan smiled reading his thoughts. 'Go home, Calder. You've earned it. In fact, go now before the orders change.'

'Are you sure?'

His friend stood and strode to the door. 'I'll escort you to the gates myself.'

Calder collected his pack with his few belongings and gladly left the uniform and weapons on the bed.

In the courtyard, soldiers lined up for inspection. Their weapons were sheathed, but it was a reminder of what the uniform stood for and the lives Calder had taken when he'd worn it. He didn't have a soldier's temperament, only his life with Arliss mattered. A life of peace untouched by the ravages of war.

'At ease soldiers!' Captain Ashan regarded the men awaiting his orders. 'Wait here. I have an announcement to make.'

Calder noted the faces of men who had once been strangers, but he was now honoured to call friends. He nodded to each in passing before walking to the exit of the castle grounds.

A smile curled his lips as he turned to Ashan, realising what the captain had given him. Freedom.

He saluted. 'Good luck, Captain Ashan.'

'Goodbye, my friend. I shall miss your intuition.'

'I hope the peace holds and you won't have need of it.'

They gripped arms before Ashan turned heel and marched back to his men.

Calder set out across Cantaya alone. Cutting onto a narrow path between the trees, he pictured home and began to whistle.

***

After two uneventful days travelling, Calder longed for company. Home was still a four-day trek and the ceaseless quiet gave him too much time to contemplate the strange sensations he'd been experiencing. The intuition as Ashan had called it. That feeling when something was amiss, or the wrongness in the air he felt before an attack.

As dusk approached, he stumbled upon a small fire in a clearing of the forest. He approached warily, but the cold drove him to seek out the lone traveller hunched by the flames.

'You're welcome to join me Calder.' The woman's soft voice surprised him. As did the fact she knew his name.

'Do I know you?' He stood opposite her, the campfire crackling invitingly between them.

Her features came into focus – middled-aged with hawklike features and long black hair sweeping around her like a dark halo. Her eyes reflected the glowing embers as her gaze bore into his soul.

The witch from the castle. The accusation was on his tongue, but he held it at bay.

'I'm Zelia. It's a cold night, please sit and enjoy some warmth.'

Calder complied as if commanded and sat opposite her. He offered her an oatcake and hunk of hard cheese he'd purchased in the last town.

'I've already eaten.' She indicated the carcass of a bird by the fire, its bones picked clean.

He ate the food and she seemed content to watch, unnerving him with her attentive silence. She poured measures of mead into two cups and handed him one.

'Where are you heading?' he asked.

Zelia sipped her drink, watching him over the rim of the cup. 'The Temple of Radiance.'

'You're a bit off track, aren't you?'

'I was waiting for you.'

'Why?' He swallowed his unease with a gulp of mead. It was sickly sweet.

She grinned, though it wasn't a pleasant look on her.

Calder took another swig, trying to avoid the woman's startling dark eyes. He sensed Zelia was a schemer and suspected she was the witch Ashan had mentioned. But if she did have the king's ear what would be her reason? Surely a mystic from the temple had no call to mix with royalty. He should walk away but the warmth of the fire kept him seated, the crackling of the logs hypnotic. He sipped the mead and stared into the flames, losing himself in their swaying dance.

'It's a beautiful night to sleep under the stars. You should lie down.' Zelia's words drifted into his thoughts. Or did he imagine her speaking, her lips didn't move.

As he lay under his blanket, a thought tugged at his mind. She hadn't answered his question.

Her reasons for waiting for him no longer seemed important, though her next words filtered through as he drifted on the edge of sleep.

'The stars led me to you.'

'Stars?' He forced open leaden eyelids and saw the twinkling of the starry sky. The glorious display of shimmering light washed over him and made his skin tingle.

'Your destiny is tied up in the stars, Calder.'

'I don't believe in destiny.' The words were a struggle to get out. Sleepiness tugged at him again, drawing him under. He relaxed back into the feeling, allowing it to consume him.

'There's a prophecy passed down through my people.' Zelia's soft voice whispered through his thoughts. '*A child born of magic and starlight will rise to rule the stars. In this child's hands lies the destiny of humanity. He who commands the stars will be all powerful - immortal in the eyes of man.*'

'That's not me,' he said, the words thick on his tongue. He opened his eyes to face her but saw only blackness.

She cackled - the harsh sound even more unsettling than his sudden blindness. He felt her shadow fall across him and smelt the sweetness of the mead on her breath as her hair tickled his cheek.

'I realise it isn't you Calder.' The words whispered in his ear and made him shiver.

Paralysed, he couldn't even flinch when she dragged a pointed nail across his forehead hard enough to draw blood.

'I cannot fathom what role you are to play, but you are bound to the child. That's why I'll be keeping a close eye on you from now on.'

'I don't believe in prophecies.' Despite the claim, his voice shook.

'But you should, it's the only thing keeping you alive tonight.' Her malevolent laugh following him down into sleep.

***

Calder awoke to the dawn chorus. He stretched and sat, groaning as the motion made his vision swim. He rubbed his temple, massaging away the lingering sleepiness. His forehead was tight, and his body prickled like tiny needles were embedded in the flesh. He washed the discomfort away with a swig from his waterskin while a memory battered at the back of his mind. Try as he might, he couldn't grasp what the feeling of wrongness meant.

Zelia seemed the obvious cause. Sat opposite him, she was preparing oats and humming to herself. It wasn't a song he recognised, and the off-key pitch sent a tremor racing through him.

All night vivid dreams of murder and death, and bodies bathed in starlight plagued him. His home had featured too though it stood empty, as cold and still as a tomb. The ominous feeling remained even upon waking.

'Sleep well?' Zelia asked with a smile that didn't touch her eyes.

He shrugged and took the bowl she offered him. The porridge was topped with berries and a sprinkle of spice, and he tasted it warily before taking a bigger spoonful. 'This is good.' The sweetness of the spice cut through the tart red berries, and the oats were smooth and creamy.

She nodded and ate her own breakfast, the atmosphere awkward between them. He remembered something about stars and prophecies, but he didn't want to prolong their meeting by asking her for a recap.

Calder scraped the bowl clean and stood, eager to be on his way. 'I can wash the cooking pan and bowls for you, I passed a stream back that way.'

'No, you should get home. You've been gone a long time.'

Calder rolled his blanket and stuffed it into his pack. 'Thank you for the fire and the food.'

'It was good to meet you at last, Calder.'

He frowned at the woman, the word witch still tumbling through his thoughts. Whether Zelia was a witch or not, she unsettled him. 'I don't see why you should be interested in me.'

'So modest. Tales of your courage reached the king. Captain Ashan said your instincts saved his men on several occasions.'

'I just read the signs. Anyone with a sharp mind could do the same.' He finished tying the string of his pack and slung it over his shoulder. He was embarrassed to recall how the wind had hissed a warning of the ambush they were walking into, and another time a sixth sense had told him about the enemy creeping up on their camp. He brushed the experiences aside, he just wanted to get home to Arliss and forget about battles and death.

'We both know that's not true, Calder. You should come to the temple with me and meet the master. I'm sure he'd been able to help you.'

'I don't need help; I just need to get home to my wife.'

'Things are changing for you; I can feel it. One day you'll appreciate how special you are, and that fate has already carved out a path for you. Come to the Temple of Radiance when you want answers.'

He walked away, glad to leave the strange woman behind.

'Goodbye Calder.' Zelia called after him. 'We will meet again.'

The words followed him as he hastened to put distance between them.

***

Work had finished for the day and the village was quiet when he walked through the street. People would be at home, families eating dinner and talking about their day, others gathered in the village's only tavern. He was glad no one was around to corner him and ask questions about the raiders.

Calder smiled picturing Arliss' surprise when he walked through the door. She'd be even more surprised when he told her of his plan to apprentice as a wheelwright again. For so long he'd resisted conforming, determined to be the master of his own destiny. The months of fighting had taught him to take responsibility and support his wife and the family they hoped to start. The future stretched out filled with possibilities and he grinned stupidly as he sneaked past her family homestead. He loved her parents as his own, but it was only right he see his beloved Arliss first.

He took the track winding from the village down through the woods.

Was she preparing dinner? He sniffed the air, even though he was too far away to tell. Remembering her freshly cooked pies made his mouth water; he'd missed her food but not as much as he missed being in her company. Arliss gave his life meaning when nothing else made sense. Her love was like a fortification surrounding him; loving her made him whole.

The long track stretched ahead. Arliss must have felt so isolated without him. So far from civilisation, from help…

An image struck him. The cold lonely cottage and the wrongness surrounding it. The night darkened as though someone had shoved a hood over his head. A scream echoed out of the past and pain slammed into him. He held his stomach, feeling the hilt of a blade and blood gushing though his fingers. He dropped to his knees and his pounding heart slowed as death stole over him.

The evening light filtered back in. Calder was on his knees with the damp foliage leaking through the fabric of his breeches. His hands were dirty having raked furrows through the earth and his cheeks were wet with tears. He tasted copper. Spitting blood from his bitten tongue, he clambered to his feet and ran towards home.

'Arliss…' her name breathed out of him, no more than a strangled whisper.

His skin prickled, but he brushed the sensation aside denying the terrible thoughts before they could take hold.

Calder broke through the trees and skidded to a stop. His home stood below but the cottage was in darkness and no smoke rose from its chimney.

'Arliss!' he called finding his voice at last.

She must be staying with her parents in the village. He didn't blame her, the place reeked of loneliness. He should have insisted she leave when he received the summons to help see off the raiders.

Slipping and sliding, he tripped over his own feet as he ran down the slope to the cottage, unease building as he noticed the neglected vegetable plot and empty animal pen.

'Arliss!' He willed her to come running out to greet him, but he knew with gut-wrenching certainty he would never see the like again.

He ran to the door and banged on the wood. The place sounded hollow and empty. He ran around to the back door and stopped dead when he saw what the building had hidden from view. A grave and a cross with ARLISS carved into it stood under the ancient apple tree.

He sank down next to the mound of earth and wept.

It was fully dark when her father discovered him at the graveside. 'Calder, I'm sorry. We tried to get word to you.'

He shook his head unable to speak.

'We sent letters hoping one might reach you. I've come here every night waiting for your return.'

'When?' Calder's voice was a barely audible croak.

Lenen put a heavy hand on his shoulder. 'Let's get you in front of the fire and find something for the shock.'

He led Calder inside. The cottage was cold and empty. He sat numbly at the table remembering the meals he'd shared with Arliss.

Lenen built a fire in the kitchen hearth. The warmth of the blaze didn't touch his skin and the burn of the liquor forced upon him was tasteless as it slid down his throat.

Lenen settled opposite him, clasping his own cup of liquor. He cleared his throat.

'Raiders came three weeks ago. Those of us not conscripted saw them off. But they'd already been here. They murdered her Calder… my little girl.'

Lenen broke down and they were both silent for a long time.

'How?' Calder asked as unwanted images filtered through his thoughts - Arliss pale as moonlight in a dark hole.

The older man knocked back the liquor and coughed. He hung his head and gazed into his empty cup. 'I found her. One fatal wound in her belly. The doctor said she didn't suffer long.'

All Calder could think about was his wife and the pain and fear she must have felt dying alone. Arliss' fate tore into his soul.

'Why did they do this?' Lenen asked.

Calder remembered the few raiders they'd managed to capture alive. He'd been appalled watching them die; now he wished he'd made them suffer, that he'd killed every one of the raiders who came to Cantaya with the intention of murdering innocent people. 'They were searching for something. The raids appear random, but they must have had a plan for coming here. I never thought she'd be in danger. If I'd known I would've ignored the conscript…'

'Treason is a hanging offence. You'd be no help to anyone dead.'

'It wouldn't matter if Arliss lived. She should be here.'

'I know, son. I'd give anything to have my daughter back. We should have insisted she stay with us while you were gone.'

Calder imagined his headstrong wife and shook his head. 'She would never agree. This was her home... our home.' Though it no longer felt like home, just a shell bereft of everything that had made it special.

'I'll leave you to get some sleep.' Lenen stood and added another log to the fire. He left the small bottle of liquor and a basket of rolls and dried beef on the table.

'I'll stop by in the morning with more supplies.' As he left, Lenen took something from his pocket and placed it on the table.

Light from the candle glinted off the metal wedding band. Pain ripped through Calder. Tears blurred his vision and he scarcely registered he was alone.

He stared at the symbol of their love for a long time. As he grasped the ring, a sob choked him.

The metal burned into his palm and the room suddenly filled with blinding light. When his sight adjusted, the kitchen was gone lost to the grey mists pulsing around him.

Calder.

Her spirit hovered above him, shimmering within the mists to become more distinct.

'Is this a dream?' He asked.

'No, my love.'

'What is this place, where are you?

'The in-between - the world between life and death. I can't pass over without your help.'

'Don't go, I can't live without you.'

'You must.' Her spirit eyes filled with tears. 'It's not your time, you have a purpose to fulfil.'

'I can't go on alone.'

'My darling this isn't the end for you. You need to help me pass over, to find my peace.'

'I don't want to lose you.'

'It's too late...'

'What if I took a dagger and drove it into my heart. Then we could be together again.'

'No!' She cried and grasped his hands. 'It'll never be enough. You have another path to follow.'

He dropped to his knees. 'How can you ask me to go on without you?'

'Because you must.'

'This is a cruelty no man should endure.'

'My love I don't understand it either, but I know you have a higher purpose, to help spirits like me find our way through. There are so many tortured souls trapped in the in-between, we need you.'

Calder's soul splintered into a thousand pieces. Even though it destroyed him, he had to let her go.

She pulled him to his feet. 'Promise me you'll live Calder.'

'I can't make that promise.'

'Please.'

He considered the bleak future stretching ahead of him. 'I will live for you, but it will not be living. Nothing will be the same without you.'

'You will have happiness again.'

'No. You were my heart and now it's broken beyond repair.'

They held one another. Arliss stroked her fingers down his cheek before pulling away. 'It's time. Are you ready?'

He wanted more than anything to stay with her even if it meant they were both trapped in the in-between. But he sensed her pain; this was no easy place to linger. 'What do I do?'

'Take my hand Calder and summon the light.'

As tears streamed down his face, Calder visualised Arliss breaking free of the shackles of his world and passing through the murk to safety and light. Strange words came to him, their meaning unclear but his body glowed with the effort and a new light formed before them.

Arliss hovered on the brink. 'You are so much stronger than you realise, Calder. Your gift will help hundreds of spirits… Goodbye my love.'

She stepped into the light and was gone.

Calder slammed back into his body and the mists evaporated like smoke into the ether. He tried to stand but a wave of nausea flooded him and he felt light-headed. Exhausted, he slumped against the table and fell asleep.

His dreams were filled with restless spirits reaching out to him, begging for his help.

***

When Lenen arrived the next morning, Calder was dressed for travel with his bags packed by the door.

'What are you doing?'

'I can't stay here. This was supposed to be the place we spent the rest of our lives together. It's not my home anymore.'

'Where will you go?'

Calder thought about Ashan and his mission to gain information on the raiders. His friend would appreciate the help, but the life of a soldier wasn't for him. Arliss' death had set him on a new path, one he neither understood nor wanted but he had to rescue those souls he could.

'I'll travel Cantaya for a while, see where life takes me.'

'Are you sure you won't stay? You're the son I never had, Calder. I don't want to lose you too.'

'This is something I need to do.'

He thought of Zelia and the Temple of Radiance. Zelia had warned him things were changing. Had the mystic woman already known Arliss was dead? Did she know about the in-between and the lost spirits he inexplicably had the power to help?

He wanted answers about his new ability and what he was supposed to do now, but the temple was the last place he wanted to go. He didn't trust the mystic woman and was not inclined to seek out guidance from the temple master either. He would find his own way.

'I'll miss you, son,' Lenen said, dragging him back to the present.

They embraced, shared pain passing between them.

'Come say goodbye to the wife. She'll be upset if you don't.'

Calder followed him out of the door. He locked up and passed Lenen the key. 'Do what you see fit with the place.'

By rights it was Lenen's anyway; Calder had offered it as a dowry when he asked to marry Arliss, intending to pay rent to live there. Lenen had agreed but gave it to them as a wedding gift instead.

Calder looked back at his old family home, thinking of all those who'd once shared it with him;

his parents, his brother, Arliss… Their memories would always be with him, he didn't need the reminders trapped in the fabric of the building.

His father-in-law didn't speak as they lugged Calder's bags between them and walked side-by-side towards the village. The prospect of life alone was daunting, but it was the only path open to him now.

Walking through the trees where he'd had the vision of Arliss' death, Calder detected the faint presence of other spirits. They were fleeting impressions of people long dead and forgotten, too far gone to help. But there were others out there like Arliss who needed him. Thinking of her firmed his resolve, even though another piece of him broke inside.

'I have something for you back at the workshop, a parting gift,' Lenen said eventually. 'I fixed the old wagon. It's only right you take it. We'll buy you a mule from old Jenka. I'll be happier knowing you have a roof to sleep under and company on the road.'

'Thank you…' Calder coughed to clear emotion from his throat. 'I'd like that.'

'It's important you're not alone, son. Don't take forever coming back to us.'

He nodded though he had no idea if he'd ever return. They shared sad smiles and kept walking.

Calder remembered restoring the wagon. It had been a project they'd worked on together before news of the raiders broke. Calder may have failed to become a wheelwright and follow in Lenen's footsteps, but he did prove to have a knack for fixing things. He'd enjoyed the evenings working on it with Lenen while Arliss and her mother prepared dinner. Happy times, memories to sustain him through the dark days to come.

Calder peered at the tree shrouded sky and imagined his wife's spirit at his shoulder. He'd promised to live for her, and he would. He'd follow her last wish and help the spirits on their final journey. Maybe one day he'd be reunited with Arliss. Wherever he ended up, he would always carry her in his heart.

***

The Starlight Prophecy series is coming soon…

Praise for Suzanne Rogerson

'I've been reading fantasy and SF for over fifty years. I recognize a born story teller when I read one. Suzanne Rogerson held me spellbound. The author is destined to become a legend.' **Amazon Reviewer**

'This author has done wonderful things in the name of fantasy and it's a sight to behold.' **Amazon Reviewer**

'The author created such believable, magical worlds with wonderful characters that I didn't want it to end.' **Amazon Reviewer**

'Visions of Zarua is a terrific achievement and Suzanne Rogerson is obviously a writer to watch.' **Amazon Reviewer**

DEAR READER

I hope you've enjoyed this peek into the fantasy worlds of my novels and if you are inspired to check out the rest of the books in my back catalogue you can find everything you need on Amazon author page.

If you want to get in touch, you can use the contact form on my website. I love to hear from my readers. And if you feel so inclined, please consider leaving a short review which can really help my books get noticed. They really do make a difference to an author. They certainly brighten my day!

ALSO BY THE AUTHOR

Short Story Collections

Fantasy Short Stories
Love, Loss and Life in-between - Short Story
Collection
(COMING SOON)

Fantasy Books

Silent Sea Chronicles Trilogy
The Lost Sentinel - Book 1
The Sentinel's Reign - Book 2
The Sentinel's Alliance - Book 3
Also available as Silent Sea Chronicles Boxset

Standalone epic fantasy
Visions of Zarua

Starlight Prophecy
(COMING SOON)

Romance

The Mermaid Hotel Romance Series
(COMING SOON)

AUTHOR PROFILE

Suzanne lives in Middlesex, England with her husband, two children and a crazy spaniel. Her writing journey began at the age of twelve when she completed her first novel. She discovered the fantasy genre in her late teens and has never looked back. Giving up work to raise a family gave Suzanne the impetus to take her attempts at novel writing beyond the first draft, and she is lucky enough to have a husband who supports her dream - even if he does occasionally hint that she might think about getting a proper job one day.

An author of four novels including Silent Sea Chronicles trilogy and a Czech translation of her debut, Visions of Zarua, Suzanne hopes the dreaded 'W' word will never rear its ugly head again!

She loves gardening and has a Hebe (shrub) fetish. She enjoys cooking with ingredients from the garden and regularly feeds unsuspecting guests vegetable-based cakes. Suzanne collects books, is interested in history and enjoys wandering around castles and old ruins whilst being immersed in the past. Most of all she loves to escape with a great film, binge watch TV shows, or soak in a hot bubble bath with an ice cream and a book.

Find Suzanne on her website for information about new releases and to follow the link to join her mailing list;

www.suzannerogersonfantasyauthor.com

Twitter @rogersonsm

Instagram @suzannemrogerson

Facebook @suzannerogersonfantasyauthor

Lightning Source UK Ltd.
Milton Keynes UK
UKHW040646051222
413345UK00005B/795